D0786267

Trick or Treat, Smell My Feet

Diane de Groat

Morrow Junior Books   New York

Watercolors were used for the full-color illustrations.
The text type is 14-point Korinna.

Published by Morrow Junior Books
a division of William Morrow and Company, Inc.
1350 Avenue of the Americas, New York, NY 10019
www.williammorrow.com

Printed in Hong Kong by South China Printing Company (1988) Ltd.

3 5 7 9 10 8 6 4 2

Library of Congress Cataloging-in-Publication Data
De Groat, Diane.
Trick or treat, smell my feet/Diane de Groat.
p. cm.
Summary: Gilbert is excited about the costume he is
planning to wear in the Halloween parade at school, until he
discovers that lots of others have the same costume.
ISBN 0-688-15766-1 (trade)—ISBN 0-688-15767-X (library)
[1. Halloween—Fiction.   2. Costume—Fiction.
3. Brothers and sisters—Fiction.   4. Schools—Fiction.]
I. Title.   PZ7.D3639Tr 1998   [E]—dc21   97-32916   CIP AC

To Amanda the kid

"Look, Gilbert. I'm a ballerina!"

Lola twirled around in her tutu. "It's for Halloween," she said. "What are you going to be?"

Gilbert held up the mask he was making and said, "I'm going to be one of the Martian Space Pilots—Captain Zigg. But don't tell anyone. I don't want anybody to copy my idea."

Lola suddenly stopped twirling. "I want to be a Martian
Space Pilot, too!" she cried.

"But I just finished making your costume," Mother said.
"You wanted to be a ballerina."

"You don't have to do everything I do," Gilbert said. "Your
costume is nice, too. If I were you, I would be a ballerina."

"You would?" Lola asked.

"Sure," said Gilbert. "But I'm not you, so I'm going to be
Captain Zigg."

The next day was Halloween, and Gilbert packed his Martian Space Pilot costume into a paper bag so he could change later, at school. Lola copied him and put her pink ballerina costume into a paper bag also.

"You're too little to go to school," Gilbert said. "I'll take you trick-or-treating when I get home, OK?"

"OK," said Lola. "I'll practice." She held the bag open in front of Gilbert and said, "Trick or treat!"

"Smell my feet," Gilbert answered.

"I don't want to smell your feet."

"That's what you're supposed to say on Halloween," Gilbert said.

Lola laughed and sang, "Trick or treat. Smell my feet.
Now give me something good to eat!"

"Here's a treat," Gilbert said, and he dropped the piece
of toast he was eating into her bag.

After breakfast, Gilbert grabbed his paper bag and headed for the door. "Good-bye, Gilbert," Father called from the kitchen. "We'll watch for you in the costume parade."

Lola followed her brother and said, "I want to be in a parade, too!"

"You can come and watch," Gilbert said. "I'll wave to you. Remember, I'll be the one in the Martian Space Pilot costume."

Patty was waiting for Gilbert at the corner. "What are you going to be for Halloween?" she asked.

"Don't tell anyone," Gilbert whispered, "but I'm going to be Captain Zigg."

"I'm going to be a Martian Space Pilot, too," said Patty. "I'm going to be Admiral Zena."

"Hey," Gilbert said. "Being a Martian Space Pilot was *my* idea."

"I guess we had the same idea," Patty said. "I hope no one else does."

After lunch, Mrs. Byrd stood in front of the class and said, "Boys and girls, Principal Pines will be leading the parade today. We will all line up in the hall and then march single file out the main entrance and around the block. Stay with your class. And if you see your family or your neighbors, you may wave, but please do not leave the line. Then, when we come back to our room, we can have our party."

Everyone shouted, "Yay!"

"Now you may line up to get into your costumes," Mrs. Byrd said. *"Quietly."*

Lewis lined up behind Gilbert. He waved his monster mask in Gilbert's face and said, "Trick or treat!"

Gilbert laughed and said, "Smell my feet!"

Everyone snickered. Except Mrs. Byrd. She said, "Lewis and Gilbert, please go to the end of the line."

They were the last ones in the boys' room, and some of
their classmates were already in costumes. Gilbert counted
five Martian Space Pilots!

"I'm Captain Zigg," Frank said in a deep Captain Zigg
voice. "I've come to save your planet."

"Hey," said Gilbert. "You copied my idea! *I* was going to
be Captain Zigg."

"Well," Frank said, "it looks like a lot of us had the
same idea."

When the other boys finished dressing, they went back to the classroom. Not Gilbert. He wasn't excited about his costume anymore. He wished he had thought of something different, but now it was too late. He opened his bag.

He closed it quickly and blinked hard.

He opened the bag again. He wasn't looking at his Captain Zigg costume. He was looking at Lola's ballerina costume!

Gilbert pulled out the frilly pink tutu. "This must be some kind of trick," he said. He shook the bag, and a half-eaten piece of toast fell out. "And this is definitely *not* a treat!"

Gilbert thought a moment. If he had Lola's costume, she must have his. And she was probably wearing it right now, waiting for the parade!

Gilbert needed to get it before the party. But he didn't want Mrs. Byrd to catch him outside without a costume on. She would think Gilbert forgot to bring one, and she had already scolded him once today.

There was only one thing to do.

Gilbert undressed and pulled on the tutu, tugging it up as far as it would go. Then he picked up the paper bag and tore out two holes for the eyes. It wasn't exactly a mask, but at least it was a disguise. He didn't want his friends to see him dressed as a ballerina!

When Gilbert stepped into the hallway, his class was already passing through. No one recognized him, so he followed them down the hall and out the door. The street was lined with people watching and waving and taking pictures. Gilbert looked up and down the street, cutting in and out of line, but he couldn't find his sister anywhere.

"Hey, quit pushing!" someone yelled.

"It's not me," a tall Space Pilot said. "It's that girl with the bag on her head."

"Please stay in line," a teacher said. Gilbert recognized Mrs. Byrd's voice behind him. Then he heard another voice he knew.

"Look, Daddy—Gilbert's wearing my ballerina costume!"

Up ahead, he saw Lola standing next to Father, and she was wearing Gilbert's costume.

"Hey, Gilbert!" she called, and waved.

Gilbert looked around to make sure Mrs. Byrd couldn't see him leave the line. Then he rushed over to Lola.

"I need my costume! Quick!" he shouted.

"Gimme mine first," she said.

"Stay with your class, boys and girls," a teacher said loudly. Gilbert grabbed Lola's hand and pulled her back toward the line with him.

Lola thought she was going to be in the parade with the big kids, but Gilbert pulled her right through the line and headed for the school. "Hey, where are we going?" she asked.

"Someplace where we can switch costumes," Gilbert said. He knew that the side door was a shortcut to the bathrooms. "Quick," he said. "This way!"

But Lola wasn't very quick. She kept tripping over the too-big costume. By the time they reached the boys' room, they were out of breath. Gilbert pushed the door open and there was Lewis, standing in his underwear. "Hey! No girls allowed," Lewis yelled.

"Let's try the girls' room," Lola said helpfully.

"No way," Gilbert said. "Come on—maybe my classroom is still empty!"

They ran down the hall to Mrs. Byrd's room. They had just reached the door when Lola tripped on her costume—and Gilbert tripped on Lola. They tumbled inside, right into the middle of a party!

Gilbert's paper bag mask had flown off. Everyone was staring at him—and his tutu.

Gilbert did the only thing he could think of. He twirled around the room, then raised his arms up and said, "Ta-da!"

There was a long silence. "Gilbert?" Frank asked finally. "What are you supposed to be?"

"He's a ballerina, silly," Lola said as Mrs. Byrd helped her to her feet. "And I'm Captain Zigg."

Patty said, "Well, Gilbert, at least you didn't have the same costume as everyone else."

"Of course not," Gilbert said. "I wanted to be something different. My sister here wanted to be a Space Pilot like everyone else. But not me," he said proudly. Then he twirled across the floor to the refreshment table.

Soon Father appeared at the door to take Lola home. Mrs. Byrd gave her some pumpkin cookies to take back with her. "Trick or treat," Mrs. Byrd said, handing her the bag.

"Smell my feet," Lola said, taking it.

She passed Gilbert on the way out. "Are you still going to take me trick-or-treating later, Gilbert?"

"I guess so," he said.

"And Gilbert?"

"What?"

"This time can *I* be the ballerina?"

Gilbert laughed. "Don't you want to be a Martian Space Pilot anymore?"

"No," she said, taking Father's hand. "If I were you, I'd be one, but I'm me, so I'm going to be a ballerina." She skipped out the door singing…

TRICK OR TREAT,
SMELL MY FEET.
GIVE ME SOMETHING
GOOD TO EAT!